MONKEY & ROBOT

FLIGHTS OF FANCY

PETER CATALANOTTO

To Amy and Norm, for loving my daughter as their own.
A special thank you to JoEllen.

Cover and internal design by Simon Stahl

Library of Congress Control Number: 2021946706

Published by Creston Books, LLC
www.crestonbooks.co

ISBN 978-1-954354-04-3
Source of Production: 1010 Printing
Printed and bound in China
5 4 3 2 1

CONTENTS

Spider Monkey 7

Almost Famous 23

Turtles in the Mist 38

Cookie Time 53

Monkey, bring your chalk inside. It looks like rain.

SPIDER MONKEY
Where is the aquarium?
In the basement. Why?
I have a plan.
For what?
To become a superhero.

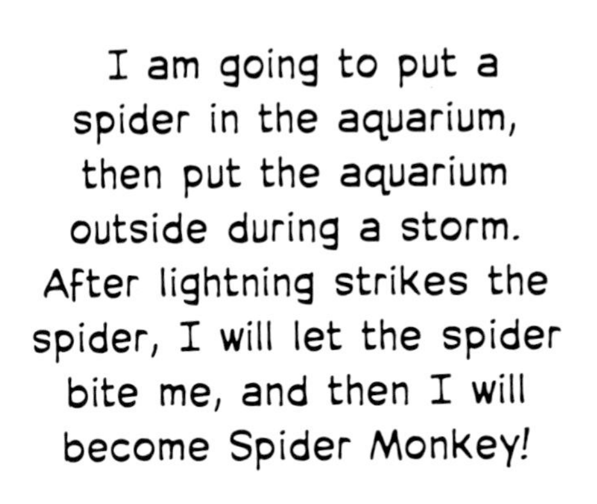
I am going to put a spider in the aquarium, then put the aquarium outside during a storm. After lightning strikes the spider, I will let the spider bite me, and then I will become Spider Monkey!

Wow, that is quite a plan.

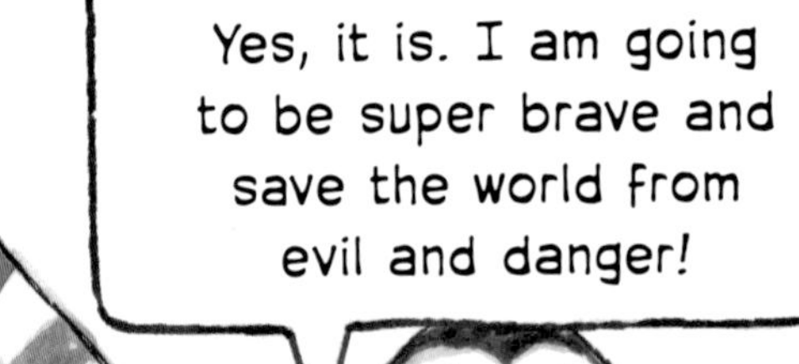
Yes, it is. I am going to be super brave and save the world from evil and danger!

But there is one small problem.
What is that?

I am afraid of spiders.
That is a problem.

I am afraid of storms, too.
Well...

Oh, and now I am also afraid of going into the basement to find the aquarium.

Will you come with me?
Absolutely.

Monkey and Robot found the aquarium.
Now we need a smaller container to catch the spider.
Like this?
Perfect!
Will you help me catch the spider?
Of course. What kind of spider do you need?
I think any spider will do.
Okay, let's look behind the oil tank.
Robot peeked behind the oil tank.
Wow! There is a huge spider back here!
Quick! Hand me the cup!
Monkey?

Monkey?
I am upstairs!
I need the cup!
CUP!

Robot scooped up the spider.

Wow, it *is* gigantic!

A clap of thunder shook the house.
KABOOM!
EEEEEEEK!
Perfect timing! Let's get the aquarium outside.

How about here?
Is this a good place, Monkey?
Monkey?
Robot set the aquarium on the front walk. He ran back into the house.
Monkey?
MONKEY!
I am in my room!
What is the matter?
I figured out one more problem with my plan.
I really do not want that spider to bite me!

It's okay, Monkey. You do not have to do it.
But I want to be a superhero who saves everyone!
KA-BOOM!
Rain pelted the window.
Oh dear. The spider is trapped out there.
Can you let it out of the aquarium?
No. I will rust if I go out in the rain.
I can throw my rolled-up socks from the front door and knock the top off of the aquarium.

Ten minutes later...

Those are all the socks you own.
Bring me my underwear!
Monkey, the aquarium is getting water in it. The spider will drown.
Call the police! Call the fire department! *Call the Marines!*
There is no time. You must free the spider now.
You can do it.

EEEEEEEEEEEEEEEEEEEEEEEEEEEEEEEEEEEEEEEEEEEEEEEEEEEEEEK!

SLAM!
You did it! You saved the spider! You are a superhero!
No, I am not. I was not brave. I was terrified the entire time!
Monkey, being brave when you are afraid is the bravest brave of all!
It is?
Yes.

KNOCK! KNOCK! KNOCK!
It's the spider!
Who is it?
It's the police.
Your neighbor called. She heard a lot of screaming.
Oh, that was just me being a superhero.

Soooooo...
everything
is okay?
Oh yes, officer.
We are sorry
to have
bothered you.
You are very
brave to be out
in this storm.
I'm just doing
my job. Have a
good evening.
As the police officer closed the
door, Monkey and Robot saw
the spider on his collar.

EEEEK!
See? You can be very brave and afraid at the same time.
Indeed. Now let's get you into a dry cape.
Well, if being afraid is being brave, I must be the greatest superhero of all time!
The End

ALMOST FAMOUS

Hmm.
Let's take pencils and paper with us to the park.
Great! I can practice my autograph!
Well, I thought we could write down ideas for becoming famous.
Okay, but after we eat. When I am hungry, I can only think about food.
On their way to the park, Monkey and Robot saw a boy crying.

What is wrong?
Oh dear.
Mew!
Do not worry. My friend Monkey is an excellent climber. He can have your kitten down in...

Here you go.
Lulu!
Mew.

Great job, Monkey!
Thanks. Let's go. I am really hungry!
At the park...
Monkey ate a peanut butter and banana sandwich and two chocolate-frosted peanut butter banana cookies.
Mmmm. Okay, I am ready to think. What can I do to be famous?

Let's start with things you love to do. Then, even if you do not become famous, you will still be doing something you love!
Well, I love to eat, I love to play, and I love being at the park with you!
Which one is the fastest way to become famous?
They tried to think of ideas. Neither of them noticed their paper was blowing away.
You know, Monkey... some people who become famous don't like it.
Why?

Maybe at first. But imagine every day, everywhere you go, lots of people want your autograph and to take pictures with you. People would bother you wherever you go and whatever you do.

People in the park noticed Monkey and Robot's papers blowing around and collected them.

People would bother me when I am playing?
Yes.
People would want to take pictures with me when I am eating?
Yes.
People would ask me for autographs when I am sitting in the park with you?
Yes.

That is terrible!
I do not want that!
Excuse me.
AAAAAAAAAH!
PLEASE LEAVE ME ALONE! I NEED TIME TO EAT, TO PLAY, AND TO TALK WITH MY BEST FRIEND!
IT IS ALL TOO MUCH! I CAN'T TAKE ANY MORE!

Please, I just want to be left alone.
Thank you so much.
sob
It's okay now, Monkey, it's okay. Everyone has left.
sniff

Monkey and Robot packed their picnic basket and folded their blanket. On their way home...

Please leave me alone!
I do not want to sign any autographs!
I do not want your autograph.
You don't?
No. I want to give you these coupons for saving our kitten this morning.
They are from the ice cream shop my husband and I own in town. You can have free ice cream all week.

You are both heroes. Thank you! Thank you!
Wow.
Isn't it nice to be recognized for doing something good?
It is delicious!
I wish I could be just a little famous instead of really famous.
Monkey noticed a small group of people walking towards them.
Oh no!

It will be okay, Monkey...watch.
Excuse me. Would any of you like Monkey's autograph?

No, thank you.

FREE
FREE
Hooray!
I am only a little famous!

See! Everything is okay.

Off we go now.
That is the wrong way.
We live this way.
But the ice cream lives *this* way!
Of course. Silly me.
The End

TURTLES IN THE MIST

Oh, yes! We could study them and then write our own book about the amazing things we learn.

I like that idea!

I have another idea... wait here!
Ten minutes later:
TA-DA!
Wow! You are a box turtle!
Rats. I am trying to be a real turtle.
A box turtle is a real turtle.

Where would a turtle get a box?
They are called box turtles because when they pull in their head and legs, there are flaps on their lower shell that they can close to cover themselves completely.
My shell has flaps, too! I will move among the turtles and study them up close. They will not even notice me.
I will discover things about turtles that nobody else knows!
You already have a shell.
CLUNK!
CLUNK!
But our shells are too bright. We can use mud and leaves to camouflage them.
I would rather not get my shell all muddy.
I will watch and write notes. I will take pictures, too.

Robot gathered a camera, a notebook, and a pencil. The two friends headed into the woods.
Everything is so wet from the rain.
There is the pond!
Okay, you stay here while I sneak...
BONK!

Ouch.
Are you okay?
Yes, but I cannot get up.
Here.
My shell did not protect me very well.
Remember, to protect their heads, turtles pull them into their shells.
Done!
To the pond!
But Monkey, when a turtle has its head in its shell, it does not...

...walk.
BONK!
Of course.
Can you help me up again?
Can we poke holes in the front of my shell so I can see when my head is protected?
Yes! But first take off your shell so I do not stick you with the pencil.

I cannot take my shell off, Robot. Then everyone will see I am not a real box turtle.
We are still far enough from the other turtles. You can hide behind the tree.
Oh, no. I am not going near *that* tree.
It will only take a minute.
I would really rather not.
Okay, then no walking with your head inside your shell.
But look, your shell is rounder. Plus with the leaves and mud on it...
...it looks more like a real turtle shell.
Really? Take a picture so I can see!

Monkey and Robot gathered leaves.

I am all set. Now I will creep very slowly to the pond, blend in with the other turtles...
...and learn so much about their turtle ways.
Oh, dear.
Monkey?
Shhhhh.

Monkey!
Now I see why you did not want to take your shell off to make eyeholes.
Please write in the notebook: trees do not like turtles.
That is certainly something most people do not know.
Look! By your foot!
Well, hello there.

It thinks you are its mother.
That is apparent!
Robot, I know a mother is a parent.
No, I meant...
Never mind. I think it wants food. We should find a worm to feed it.
Ugh. That is not very nice.
Turtles love to eat worms!
Then it is not very nice for the worm!
Ooh, here is a big one! You can use a stick to pick it up.
I will take pictures.

I cannot do it!
It is too mean!
Ack!
SPLAT!

Oof!
STOP IT, TREE!
WE ARE NOT REAL TURTLES!
Thank you.
I think that is enough research for today.
Let's go home and wash up for dinner.
Can we take it home? I will name it Pokey. It can live in our aquarium.

It might have a family who will wonder where it is.
Just one night? We can bring it back in the morning. Please?
Okay.
Just for tonight.
Come here, little one.
Oh.

Later that night...
POKEY
WORMS
Now that we are experts on worms, tomorrow morning we should place Pokey near some decaying leaves to eat.
Good idea. But we do not have to dress up as worms when we take Pokey home, do we?
Hmmm.
The End

COOKIE TIME

I think I will have a chocolate-frosted peanut butter banana cookie.

You ate the last one yesterday.

I know.

Then you know you cannot have one.

We will see about that. Follow me.

Oh?

On the back porch...
Ta-da!
The box?
It's a time machine!
I turned my old tricycle upside down and attached it to a clock. I will pedal backwards to last week when there was a plateful of cookies.

I see. You know I will bake more on Saturday.
Do not worry, I will eat all of those, too.

Maybe more than once!

Um...okay. Good luck!
Please close the door!
KNOCK! KNOCK! KNOCK!
Coming!
KNOCK! KNOCK! KNOCK!
Oh, hello, Ms. Harper.
Hello, Robot.
Would you kindly look at my crock pot? I cannot get it to work.
Of course. I can do it now. Come back in an hour.
Wonderful! Thank you! Thank you!

Hmm.
Robot turned the crock pot upside down and saw he needed a screwdriver to open the panel.
The tool kit is in the basement.
WARNING
Do not open
(unless you are a robot)
On the back porch...
There!
That should do it!
Cookies, here I come!

Oh no! I went back way too far! Robot is just a baby!

Hello, baby Robot. I am Monkey. When you grow up, we are going to be best friends and have lots of fun and adventures. But now I must return to my time machine and go back, I mean, go forward, to when you are grown up. See you soon!

Oh dear. These screwdrivers are all too big.
I need the small screwdriver set under the kitchen sink.
Aha!
When Robot lifted the fire extinguisher, the lever pressed against the pipe.
SSSSSSHHOOOOOSH!
Oh dear.

Meanwhile, Monkey was convinced he had pedaled forward in time enough for Robot to no longer be a baby.
He burst into the house and saw Robot stumble out of the kitchen.
Monkey? Are you there? I can hardly see!
Monkey?
Oh, no! I have traveled way too far into the future! Now Robot is really old!
Let me help you, old Robot.
Sit here. Rest your weary bones. I will fix this!

Back to the time machine!
Thank you, Monkey. Would you please bring me a towel?
Monkey?
Monkey, where are you?
I must get this right!
I do not want Robot to be a baby...
...and I do not want him to be really old, either!

Sigh.
Ms. Harper will be here shortly, and I have not even opened the crock pot!

Ah, here is the problem.
A loose wire.
There! That should do it.
Success!
KNOCK! KNOCK! KNOCK!
KNOCK! KNOCK!
Coming!

Hello, Ms. Harper. Your crock pot is ready to use again.
Wonderful! I knew you could fix it!
Here, I baked these as a thank you.
Chocolate-frosted peanut butter banana cookies... our favorite!
Thanks again!

Whew.
That should do it.

Robot! Hurray! You are not a baby or really old!
Cookies!
I did it! I did it!
I went back just the right amount of time. Back to when there were cookies!

Well...
You do not know what I am talking about because I do not show you my time machine until next week!
Mmmm...they are still warm. My timing was perfect!
Monkey, those are new cookies.
Yes, they are... to you!
But, Monkey, you never actually...
Robot saw how proud Monkey looked.
I never what, Robot?
You never...
Sigh. You never cease to amaze me, Monkey.
The End